MR. G_____E

Roger Hargreaves

Original concept by
Roger Hargreaves

EGMONT

Mr Grumble's name suited him well!

"Bah!" he would grumble, every morning, when his alarm clock rang.

"It's the start of yet another horrible day!"

"Bah!" he would groan, every afternoon, on his walk in the country.

"I hate the countryside!"

One day, just after he said this, someone suddenly appeared by magic.

It was a wizard.

A wizard, to whom Mr Grumble had the nerve to say, "Bah! I hate wizards who suddenly appear by magic."

"Really?" said the wizard. "Well, I don't like people who are constantly grumbling and moaning. I'll tell you what I do to people who have bad manners. I turn them into …

… little pigs!"

And the wizard disappeared, leaving behind him a very piggy-looking Mr Grumble.

Mr Grumble was afraid that he might remain a pig for the rest of his life.

But five minutes later, by magic, of course,
he changed back into his old self.

He set off again, and happened to pass Little Miss Fun's house.

"Come in!" she cried.

"I'm having a party!"

Mr Grumble went in, but when he heard Little Miss Fun's guests singing and laughing, he scowled.

"Bah!" he moaned. "I can't stand singing and laughing!"

He would have done better to have kept quiet, because …

… the wizard appeared once more.

"I see that my first lesson wasn't enough!" he said.

"If I'm going to teach you to stop grumbling, groaning and moaning, I'll have to do more than turn you into a little pig, I'll have to turn you into …

… a big pig!"

Mr Grumble did not like it one bit.

Little Miss Fun and her guests, however, found it very funny.

"Please," begged Mr Grumble, "turn me back to normal! I promise that I will never grumble, groan or moan ever again!"

And he feebly wiggled his curly tail.

The wizard took pity on him, and changed him back to his old self.

And then the wizard disappeared again.

Then Little Miss Fun jumped on to a table and pretended to be a clown.

Mr Grumble was not amused.

"Bah!" he snorted. "I can't stand people who jump on to tables and pretend to be clowns!"

You can guess what happened next.

He turned into …

… an enormous pig!

An enormous pig whose face was red with embarrassment!

"Oink!" wailed Mr Grumble, mournfully.

Then, this enormous red-faced pig made a solemn promise.

"Never again will I grumble, groan, moan or snort!"

"Good," said the wizard, suddenly appearing once again.

And Mr Grumble changed back into his old self.

Well, not exactly his old self!

Look at that nice smile on his face!

Amazing, isn't it?

Later, Mr Grumble went home.

And, tired out after his exhausting day, he went straight to bed.

He slept the whole night without once grumbling, groaning, moaning or snorting.

But not without …

… snoring!